FLEETING GLANCES

ASHMITA CHAKRABORTY

Contents

Preface

*Satya, a traveler who explored the length and breadth of India, was known for his
charming and Well Educated .*
But as fate would have it, everything changed when he set foot in Hyderabad.
*In the midst of his journey, he laid eyes on Preeti, a college girl, and his heart
skipped a beat.*
*For the first time, Satya experienced the enchanting feeling of falling head over
heels in love.*
*Preeti, a diligent student, had a passion for helping others, making her even more
captivating to Anup.*
*Their paths intertwined, creating a beautiful love story that would forever be
etched in their memories.*

Acknowledgements

I wish to thank Srimedhi Didi , Whose small Glimpses form
the basis of this novel♡
The whole story is Mixed Vision
Of fiction and non-fiction .
Thank you ♡

Quotes

"

If the Love is pure , then the soul will reborn again & In next birth , the Love story will be Complete."

CHAPTER ONE

PLANNING FOR THE ADVENTURE

Dehradun: Dehradun is the capital and the most populous city of the
Indian State of Uttarakhand. Dehradun ' s nickaname Is Doon because it is
located over Doon Valley . Also known as Abode Droana
Dehradun is famous for Tapkeshwar Temple , Indian Military, Doon Valley
and so more.
It is considered to visit dehradun in April , June , October as the
temperature normally falls between 20 -25° Celsious .

.

Satya (main Character) he losts his father in a car accident . He has only his
mom & uncle in the name of family. He has a passion or can say Dream of
Travelling along the cities . He completed his Graduation with distinction
but as has a passion Of travelling . So, he wanti to travel but without her
mom's permission he can't go .
He had asked his mom for thrice to fourth times but his mom refused as
she feels if the same happens with her son then who will take care of her
how she will live the whole life . After Passing 3 months , Satya asked the
same again to his mom but this time satya promised his mom that he will
call her and take care of his own self . His mom was quit not agreed but
convinced .
Satya, packing his bags And foods like chips , biscuits & water .

Satya's mom was emotional but not showing her feelings in front of Satya
as well as Satya is also emotional but not showing in front of his mom if he
shows his feelings then his mom will stopped

him to travel again.
Satya , takes blessings of his mom and uncle and sat in car . He was ready to
leave .
His uncle Timothy says, come back soon dear .
Take care of yourself. Bye !
Satya leaves with his blue car .
(The day was 17 th September at 3PM)
Satya, On the way to Delhi at first , he was emotional because he was
leaving his place where he has born , studied, makes friends & relatives. He
notices a old man , he stopped his car and helped the old man . He has
given lift to the old man .
Old man says, where are you going Dear ?
Satya , I'm leaving doon uncle
Old man , is it here you born ?
Satya, yes I grew up here .
Old man , so why are you leaving ?
Satya , For Passion , we need to leave the past to achieve future
Old man , true my dear
Old man , stopped the car here
Satya stopped his car and goodbids old man.
Old man , I blessed you dear you will be so much happy in yours life.
Satya , thank you uncle will meet again and leave .
After crossing the checked pass he stopped his car near the café .
He parked his car and went there to drink a cup of coffee . He drank and

*while leaving he meets his friend Georgia ,
Satya, hello Georgia
Georgia , hey where are you going ? Are you
leaving today ?
Satya, yeah what about you how you are here ?
Georgia, I am good , I came here with my Dad .
Georgia leaves , Satya come to his car and he is
still in dehradun. He starts
his car and it's 6PM . He about to leave
dehradun , he calls his mom*

*Mom : Where you are ? Did you are something?
Satya, no I didn't ate . I had already leaves
about Enter delhi.*

*And cut his phone call .
Stopped his car . He rests for a minute and had
dinner . As he was sleepy so
he had taken a nap.*

CHAPTER TWO

ADVENTURE BEGINS

Delhi : Delhi is a large and Sophisticated City. This city comprise , of
several elegant gardens every and trees the pollution. It is located near
the river Jamuna . The people living here belong to several different
cultures and religions.
It is seperated old & new Delhi . It is popularly for Taj Mahal , India Gate,
Jama masjid, Birla temple , gurudwara and so more.
It is considered to visit Delhi in March, October & November as the
temperature normally falls between 20-25°Celsious .
Entered Delhi ,

It's a beautiful day , the city it fills with green trees and waters .
Satya is hungry ...
He had Breakfast for the first time in Delhi .
He had Paratha and Chole
Bhature which is famous in Delhi & Packed Chicken Butter Masala n
Paratha.
He had taken a hotel for staying and he asleep in the bed when he awake it
was evening . He ordered foods to his room . He had dinner . And stays in
his room a whole night . In the nextday early morning, he goes for a walk
and a car was coming in speed , a child of 4years was in front of the car . He
rans fasts and save the child but in his hand he had a small injury. The child's parents taken Satya to their home and the child's parents were a
good nature .
They injuect Satya as child parents (both) of them are doctor .
Child parents (madhvi & sanky)
Madhvi says, You should stay here with us today
Satya, No itsokay
Sanky , yeah you stay here ,if not then tell where should I have to dropped
you ?
Satya , it's not needed , I can go by own
Sanky , No how should I can give a permission

to leave you alone in this
situation?
Satya , actually I'm from dehradun I am a
traveller , I came yesterday in
delhi.
Sanky , okay ,what do you do in dehradun?
Satya , I had graduated and I'm a scholar but
as I had a passion from young
my dad always told me whatever I wanted to do
in my life I can do it . So, I
followed it.
Sanky , okay what yours father di ? sure he will
feel very proud that you
didn't think of yours life second times to save
ours child .
Satya , yeah I'm also sure but my dad is no
more.
Sanky and madhvi in emotional
Sanky , I'm sorry but we wouldn't asks you how
yours dad dies ?
But we can say , you should stay here today
(both sanky & madhvi)
Satya, No actually I had to leave tommorow for
Nagpur as my destination
for 3 month is Hyderabad then Chennai . So, I
thought if I'm going to
Hyderabad why not Stays in Delhi and Nagpur
. This way, I will also get to
know about many things of my Indian cultures
.
Sankya : that's Wonderful.
Madhvi , okay we will not stopped you but you
have to lunch with us .

Satya, okay that's fine
They had lunch together and Satya good bids
sankya, madhvi and their
child Rohan.
He visits delhi famous places and enjoyed there
.

He Returned to his Hotel & packed his stuffs in
bag .

CHAPTER THREE

DRIVED TO NAGPUR

*Nagpur is the third-largest city of the Indian state of Maharashtra after
Mumbai and Pune.[15] Known as the "Orange City", Nagpur is the 13*
th
*largest city in India by population.
Nagpur is also known for the
Deekshabhoomi, which is graded an A-class
tourism and pilgrimage site, the largest
hollow stupa among all the
Buddhist stupas in the world.Nagpur has
tropical wet and dry climate (Aw
in Köppen climate classification) with dry
conditions prevailing for most of
the year. It receives about 163 mm of rainfall
in June. The amount of
rainfall is increased in July to 294 mm.
Gradual decrease of rainfall has
been observed from July to August (278 mm)*

and September (160
mm).[62] The highest
Recorded daily rainfall was 304 mm on 14
July 1994.[67] Summers are
extremely hot, lasting from March to June,
with May being the hottest
month. Winter lasts from November to
February, during which
temperatures occasionally drop to 10 °C (50
°F).[62] The highest recorded
temperature in the city was 47.9 °C on 29
May 2013, while the lowest was
3.5 °C on 29 December 2018.

Satya enteted nagpur .
The Night stays in a hotel .
Next day , He visits an orphanage and He
makes small memories with the
students and children's. He had been played
with few childrens and had
prepared food just like a picnic with the
orphanage childrens .
There Satya meets Tanya , She is a flirtious girl
.She has fell for Satya in her
first sight . Satya turned back and Tanya was
behind him he was about to
fall on Tanya .
Tanya says , Hey How are you ?Satya says ,
Whose this ?

Tanya Replies " I'm Tanya, what's your name ?, leave it I know your name
.."
Satya , Then why are you asking ? You're quite mad .
Tanya says , haha that's I know , Can We be friends ?
Satya replies yeah , obviously.
Tanya Replies , okay where do you stay ?
Satya " For now , I am staying in hotel .
Tanya , Why ? If you don't have problem you can come my home for
staying .
Satya , No I'm fine . I am here for few days .
Tanya , Okay ! Anyway what's yours plan for today ?
Satya, I will visits another orphanage and if I get time then will visits schools
and old brigade Home .
Tanya , you love helping , your nature is solovely I'm falling for you .
Satya , haha I had a wish even my dad had wish to help people and as he is
no more . So, I'm continuing my dad 's Wishes
.
Tanya , Oh sorry ! It's fun to help ... Okay .
Satya , Ah , I'm getting late ..
Tanya Replies , I'm helping you to serve this foods .Satya, thanks Tanya .
After serving the foods ,
Tanya Replies Satya , Can I go with you ?
Satya why not , you can come with me .
Tanya and Satya good bids the childrens and

leaves the orphanage.
Satya Was seeing Tanya as a friend but tanya
Makes this a love story .
Satya And Tanya Visits an another orphanage
& then Satya Tanya both
visits in old orohanagr . They entered , Satya
helps old woman who
wasabout to fall by slipped and Tanya saves an
old man who was About to
burn his hand . They both blessed by the old
people and few old couple had
been blessed them by couple .
Tanya heared the blessings " Old woman says ,
Hope their future would be
great they will be happy with each other "
Tanya blushed
And about to call Satya but Satya has heared
the blessings of old woman
that's why Satya leaves the orphanage and
came out . Tanya felt stranged !
After few minutes, Tanya leaves and asks Satya
, What happened to you ?
Why you came so fast as you had another plan
?
Satya replies , Nothing . I'm getting late . I will
drop you please give me
yours address . Tanya , sits and she has locked
her mouth. Tanya instructs
and directions Satya , to reach her home .
FFrom that day, Satya Was trying to ignore her
as Satya feels Tanya came
Closed to him and it is not good for his .
Next day, she comes in front of him . Satya,

Hey ! How do you know that I will be here ?
Tanya , I was tracking yours phone .
Satya , Okay ! I was about to leave for visiting schools .
Tanya , can I go with you ?
Satya , No better to focus on yours work . I don't want to disturbed you !
Tanya , o please you think this is a disturb no , It's a love , I love you Satya
Satya, please don't crack this types of jokes I don't like it .
Tanya , it's not a joke Satya . I really feel it . When I saw you first time I feel
for you ! But still I was confirmimg myself that I was true or wrong . But I
was true , I'm true .
Satya, If it's in real then I will obviously reject you . I don't love you and you
can forced me to love you. And one side love is empty box . I don't want to
loose yours career better to focus yours career you had a great future
Tanya Please leave me !
Tanya, I will realise you the love . And you have to love not by force ..i will
wait for the day .
Satya , I'm here for two days only . I'm a traveller Tanya .
Tanya, So what ? I can also go with you .
Satya , denies and leaves with his Bags .
Tanya, you can't leave without reply Satya .
Satya , bags were on car and locked the car and he went the school .

*He Visits the teacher and students . Lots of fun
he had and he good bids the
school and back to his car and ready to leave
nagpur and in mirror he saw
Tanya with her car. She was following Satya
and she hardly tries to stopped
him .
Satya , leaves for Hyderabad by confussed
Tanya . Tanya Was emotional and She tries to
find Satya but she had not even idea
where Satya is and will go....*

CHAPTER FOUR

TRAVEL TO HYDERBAD : LOVE IN THE AIR

Hyderabad: is the capital and largest city of the Indian state of
Telangana. It occupies 650 km2 (250 sq mi) on the Deccan Plateau along
the banks of the Musi River, in the northern part of Southern India.
The name Hyderabad means "Haydar's City" or "Lion
City", .Heavy rain from the south-west summer monsoon falls
between June and October, supplying Hyderabad with most of its
mean annual rainfall.Hyderabad has a tropical wet and dry
climate bordering on a hot semi-arid climate
.

Satya Enters Hyderabad. As he stepped to Hyderabad his car was on traffic.
It is morning 11:30AM it's a hot day .
Satya Saw a girl who were Pink Dress and a white scarf. She is Preeti .
Preeti (character) : preeti has parents in the name of her family . Her father
is a Good Teacher . He was posted in Dehradun and the teacher of Satya .
Her father Rakesh was a good Person with

heart . Her mom is an house wife

Rakesh has always a wish when he saw satya in childhood " Satya To make
his son" .
Satya Saw preeti and In his heart she makes a place in his first sight but he
was not confirmed that it is love or not and he was confussed about how
can he fall for someone in a first sight . He was not ready to accept but he
thinks some connection with preeti he had.
Traffic opens , he was about to cross but he was on thinking and a dog
came infront of his car . Preeti Screamed and Satya Stopped the car just like
an emergency bell .
Satya saw preeti came running infront of his car .
Preeti scolding him to not to see the dog . Satya sides car and went out
from his car and was trying to manage preeti somehow but he fails and
preeti mis understood him .
Preeti , Don't you saw the dog ?
Satya, Sorry I was thinking something
Preeti , So if you were on thinking then why don't you stop yours car on
behind .
Satya, Sorry ! I know it's my mistakes .
Preeti , it's not a mistakes , it's a sin .
Satya , I know but how can it be a sin .

*Preeti , What ?? I'm gonna complain about you
!*
*Satya hears preeti but he saw an old couple
can't crossing the road and*
*they were about to accident . So, he rans to
them for help and Preeti saw*
*this and she felt he was covering his mistakes .
Still, preeti Went to them for*
help .
*They both helped them to crossed and the old
couple blessed them .*
*Preeti to Satya , okay Now you'rr covering
yours mistakes . Huh!?*
*Do you really think I will not complain to police
.*
Satya, What ?? I'm not covering I was helping .
Preeti , stop it yours nonsense please.

*Satya , Hey listen! Whatever you will think it
will always be true that's not it*
*mean . Do whatever you want ; I already Told
you it was my mistakes still you don't*
*believe . There was my car , copy my car
number and call to police .*
Preeti , How strange !?
*Satya leaves and Went to his car and booked a
room as he will stays here*
*for 1-2 month . Also he has a wish to meet with
his Rakesh sir .*
*Before that Satya , enters for a college
proffessor. He went to the college where
preeti studies but both of them had no idea.*

Satya , enters to the college and got a professor job and he had got a professor
room for staying .
Preeti saw Satya in Staffs Room and her impression is bad with Satya form first .
Satya enteted to the classroom everyone stands and greetings to Satya .
Preeti was sitting in the left corner desk . Satya saw that and he really ignored
preeti as he is in furious . So, Satya asks questions to preeti and preeti continuosly
started Satya and in inner preeti 's mind only thinks that he came to her college
for revenge .
Satya Leaves the classroom as the bell rang and Satya punished preeti to stand in
class until the next Class starts. As soon Satya leaves preeti sat down on the bench
and after lunch she went to the cabin of Satya .
Satya was not there when preeti enters Satya leaves the staff room due to
urgency but he forget to take his car key .
Another way, Preeti saw Satya's Car key and she take it with her and she thought
to take revenge with him this way .
Satya in the parking area , he is near to his car . Preeti enters her classroom and
pretend everything fine .
Satya Rethinks and he remembers that he forget to take car key soz he back to his
staff room . Preeti completed her class she was about to give the keys to car but
as she saw that Satya was not there in parking

area . She was about to back but she rethink and she open the car and she was searching to know about Satya . And by mistake she locked herself in car . She found information about Satya's

dad and preeti's dad . She got to know about his sad past . That's make preeti Soft

corner for satya.

Preeti is in hurry to open the car but after Five times try she finally unlocked the

car and came out and locked the car becoz if Satya found preeti with his car it will

create a scene .

Unleash, preeti went to the classroom where satya gives punished preeti.

Fortunately, preeti enters to the roomm before Satya and put his key on the desk

of Satya . Satya enters to the class rom and asking to the students if his car key

found let he know and preeti standsup and told There's your key I guess.

Satya found his car key and thanks to Preeti . Satya back with his car ...

Next day is a beginning of love day ; preeti continuosly starred Satya and Satya

found it too . But he ignores, as whenever he thinks of preeti he think of his first

impression the day he met preeti.

Preeti is falling for him day by day , but now she scares to ask Satya that if he love

or not and preeti also have a doubt if her dad will agree for him or not that's why

preeti reject Satya becoz she don't want satya

to be sacrificed his passion as
preeti somewhere she gets to know that
travelling is satya's passion.
In staff room teachers were discussing about
marriage proposal and recalling
their memories and confesss to others . Satya
was confessing to others teacher
that he never fall in love until he comes to
Hyderabad and before that a girl
proposed to him but he left the city .
Satya , Hyderabad is love for me when I stepped
to Hyderabad . I saw a girl and
that day even I fought with her .
Everyone is laughing ...
Preeti heard Satya and preeti felt it and she
know how much Satya loves her.
Satya saw preeti behind the curtains and he felt
that she is falling for him and
Next day, Satya proposed to Preeti .

Preeti is in love but she still rejected Satya .
Satya , was mum and came back to his
room and got a call from dehradun his uncle
called and said " Yours mumma's
health is not well come back as soon as possible
Satya gets ready and packed his stuffs as soon
as possible and he back to
dehradun. Another way, preeti shows courage
to talk about her relationship with
Satya and preeti 's dad was in confussion as he
want her daughter happiness but
also he thinks what if she doesn't stay happy

after marriage?
Satya reached dehradun after 12hours of journey and his mom is well now but
admitted in hospital.
Here , preeti's dad gets to know about Satya and he gives permission to preeti to
marry him . Preeti found that he leaves this city and back to his city from the
teachers and takes details from every person whoever know Satya .
Preeti and preeti's dad reaches dehradun and found that Satya is in hospital and
Preeti's dad is cleared that it's the boy he had choosed to be his son .
Preeti and Satya 's parents agreed for their marriage . Satya's mom gets well .
Satya takes blessings from both of parents and was leaving for Hyderabad with
preeti .
2days later,
Preeti and Satya Reached Hyderabad with both of their parents. They had a grant
engagement ceremony but then on the next day of engaged Satya told preeti's
parents and his mom that he decides to visits Chennai . Their parents were not
agreed but they Rethinks and said you can go itsyours hobby.
Satya was leaving for Chennai but preeti stopped Satya and Preeti also want to
visit with him .so they both leave together for Chennai..

CHAPTER FIVE

TWO TRAVELLERS IN CHENNAI

Chennai : Chennai, city, capital of Tamil Nadu state, southern India, located on the Coromandel Coast of the Bay of Bengal. Known as the "Gateway to South India," Chennai is a major administrative and cultural centre.

Pop.
Satya and preeti entered Chennai . They spend times together .
Satya helped Street Childs and preeti helpes Satya . Satya visits with preeti in old orphanage and meets with few known people who came from nagpur .
Satya meets Tanya after 2months , Preeti saw Satya with Tanya .
Preeti cames to Satya , who is she sattya?
Satya, meet Tanya she is just a friend from

nagpur .
Satya to Tanya, How you came here ?
Tanya , I was searching for you and then I
becomes tired that's why , living life
with them. How you came here?
Satya, I came with my would be preeti for
spending time with her.
Preeti , hi Tanya! Nice to meet you
Tanya looks Satya 's eyes .
Tanya to Satya , how time passed na ? Like
someone doesn't care about me I
leave everything for someone and he didn't
looked up once I
Preeti to Satya , you both were close friends?
Satya , no preeti we met by an accident. Tanya
loves to visits orphan I
Preeti , oh! Okay I Shall we leave sattya

Satya invites Tanya in marriage of preeti and
satyaI
Tanya Replies by smile and in her eyes filled
with waterI
Satya and preeti leaves the orphan and spends
a beautiful time together .
Preeti Bought flowers to propose Satya . Satya
felt something in his heart and he
hugs preeti . Both visits a homeage of Rudra's
house . Satya's friend .
Rudra is married , Satya and preeti enters to
their home they had a lots of fun
and they dinner together. A call came to Satya

but as his phone is in silent that's
why nobody connects him. Preeti entered with rudra's wife room. They slept
together to discussed about future plan for career as Preeti also becoming a
Traveller by stating with Satya.
Call comes from home in preeti 's phone . Preeti picked her phone
Satya',s mom , preeti why Satya had not picked his call ? I'm in tensed
Preeti , don't worry aunty I guess he had silenced his phone and now he slept so
,I will talk to him tommorow and will told him sboutyou aunty .
Preeti 's dad , How can you both are irresponsible? We are tensed here you
both didn't call once time after leaving Hyderabad.
Preeti , Sorry I apologise you to all dad . There is a network issue. That's why I
tried to call you but it's not connected .
Satya 's mom , don't forget to call me & inform satya tommorow .
Preeti , no I will tell him don't worry sleep well. Preeti cuts the call and slept .
Next day , Satya planned to back Hyderabad as he needs to be worked on his
research that nobody knows about .
Satya called preeti ,

Satya to Preeti , We will back Hyderabad packed your stuffs .

Preeti , why are you in hurry ?
Satya , I had reasearched something 2 months before and yesterday I got a text
from unknown number they want my passcode of the research else we will be in
danger and I don't want you to be fall with me in danger.
Preeti, Satya I will not be in danger don't worry . It's just a text nothing will
happened and no need to show up yours reasearch to others.
Satya , preeti you don't know it's s risky .
Preeti , you are with me ; nothing can happen me
Satya hugs preeti .
Preeti leaves to packed stuffs , preeti in innerself she is also worried but
pretending to be nothing . In all these, preeti forgets to inform Satya that
yesterday night Satya"s mom called .
Satya and preeti Goodbids rudra .
Rudra, we will meet you soon in yours marriage.
Satya and preeti blushes and goodbids.

CHAPTER SIX

RETURNING TO HOME : TRAVELLERS DIED

Satya driving his car , Preeti slept in car as she was tired due to she hadn't

journey so long before this and Satya gets a call from his mom.

Satya'smom , you didn't call back to me once. Yesterday I call preeti at night you

slept that time she said and I am waiting for yours call from the morning .

Satya , sorry mom I am returning back to Hyderabad will be reached by night .

Satya's mom , why ? Any problem comes slowly .

Satya, no problem I have a emergency work

Satya's mom , okay .Drives slowly . We will be waiting for you

Satya cut the call and preeti awake and preeti

asks satyao if he stopped his car
for few minutes and asks for lunch in near
streets.
Satya stopped and had lunch and back to travel
again.
Satya's car gets pumptured . Satya fixed it and
their journey starts again..
It's evening 5PM , for the last time Satya talk
with his mom after that he tries to
contact but he fails .
Satya is tired and rests for few minutes.
Tanya's car was behind his car he meets
Tanya and 30 mins of gossips had snacks .
Preeti wants to buy something
Satya ,preeti and Tanya went for shopping they
brought a lot gifts for parents
and foods to eat while on journey to stay awake
. It's 8PM , preeti requested Tanya to comes
with Satya in Hyderabad.
Tanya accepts their both requests and tanya
were on her car she is following
Satya's car as she doesn't know about satya's
address .
Tanya kand Satya starts both the car and both
were in traffic but they are in 1km
difference. Satya on his way and stopped his
car becoz tanta following him.
Here, Preeti gets Littile jealous of behaviour
Satya to Tanya but preeti belives
Satya so, she keeps mum.
There was a truck behind the satya's car and a
truck was also coming from front
satya slow down his car and he want to sides

*his car and tanya's car was 1km
difference.
Satya's car had a accident. Car has broked no
parts remained.
Satya Tries to save preeti and he successfully
saved her for few hours but she
became unconscious and Satya has saw preeti
for last time .
Tanya saw the accident but can't do nothing as
the truck passed and satya's
body is filled with bloods . Tanya runned to
Satya to save but she failed .
Tanya has no idea what she will do how to save
them . Tanya runs to preeti .
She fails to awake preeti too.. she seems for
helps from others people..
They helps to carry Satya and preeti to tanya's
car.
Tanya is totally breaked she admitted both of
them . Tanya admitted Satya
near satya's friend house . Satya's friend was
there in the hospital and he saw
Satya and got to know about Satya and preeti's
accident he calls Satya's mom .
Satya 's mom and preeti's parents reached to
The hospital .
Tanya meet Satya's parents.*

*Doctors replies that Satya is no more..and
Tanya is alive but don't know the
situation . As preeti goes through the
heartbresk and she recalls her memories*

with Satya ..
Satya 's mom and uncle came to goodbids him
for last time . Satya's mom , he
yesterday says goodbids mom will come soon .
If I know this will happens , then I
will not say goodbids to Satya. I always told
him , to not go he didn't heared me
.

History is repeating again...
Preeti is admittedAdd Chapter in hospital she
knew that Satya is no more but she controls
her emotions to herself and after two days of
satya's death preeti's heart
beeped stopped and when her parents comes to
meet her she is not more .
Tanya is in trauma as she loses her parents at
first now she lost her first love
though it was incomplete but love is always love
.

And Preeti gives a responsibility to Tanya to
take care of her and satya's family.

....
After 6 months of Satya and preeti's death .
Satya's mom had died due to
mental Condition.

....

CHAPTER SEVEN

RESPONSIBILITY OF TANYA

Tanya calls daddy to Preeti's dad and Preeti's parents forget about preeti and
now Tanya is their daughter and now they leave in nagpur where Tanya used to
stay .
Tanya to Daddy, If satya and preeti is present I don't think they will give you
permission to come with me .
Daddy, yeah they were in my heart . I will always missed them .
Preeti's mom thinks it's all fault is Satya if he didn't love preeti then preeti will
not fall for him and if that time preeti's dad rejects Satya then preeti will stay
alive today and she can't accepts Tanya . So , preeti's mom stays in dehradun.
Tanya , daddy mumma will not accept me .you should go to visit mumma .
Tanya 's daddy leaves .

Tanya leaves for University as she want to continue her study and her dream to become IAS.

Tanya started preparing for upsc as she had graduated in humanities. So, preeti's dad suggests to gives upsc. Tanya had admission in college for upsc.

Tanya meets rajkamal he is too preparing for prelims. He helps Tanya soo much in her studies to pursue. Tanya bought books and she was not interested in economy as she had no ideas about it. Tanya studies with rajkamal and rajkamal is experts in economy.

She is good student but she recalls her pasts that's why she used to fails in exams

In the 5 th tests Tanya got high marks in the classes and rajkamal feels happy to see Tanya 's happiness.

Rajkamal is falling for her day by day more n more but he didn't had any ideas about Tanya 's pasts.

Tanya makes friends from the batch and rajkamal is her bestfriend from that day as he helps her . Tanya shares everything to rajkamal and from that day Tanya stopped recalling her pasts . It's seems she forgets everything and started moveon.

Tanya topped in every tests , on upsc prelims she had done a try to get good marks and she thinks she will be selected and

*another way, rajkamal also had
done good .
In result day, Tanya had selected and rajkamal
hadnot selected only for 1 marks .
Else Tanya ranked 35 in all India . Rajkamal
appears next time and he selected
this times.
Tanya appeared in Mains but she failed in
mains snd that makes her demotivate
as it's her daddy's wish so , she tried hard to
full filled but in first time she failed.
Another way, rajkamal had been selected for
interview and Tanya needs helps
but this time nobody was there to help her ..
She had studied for next time and she had been
selected for mains and she
appears and selected for interview too but the
relationship between rajkamal
and Tanya becomes different as rajkamal felt in
love .but tanya has not refused
or not accept she is in dilemma.*

*Tanya cleared Interviews and rajkamal also
cleared the interview and both were
on training of 4 years .
Tanya lost his made dad . Preeti 's dad died in
a heartattack due to pressure .
Preeti has lost many things and she scares to
make relationship just because she
thinks if she makes relationship they will die ..
Preeti 's mom blame Tanya for everything.
Tanya has no more strength left after loosing*

*everyone . Now, rajkamal is in her
life . Rajkamal takes stands in her bad times
and takes responsibility of her as her
friend until she thinks her life mate .
Tanya tried again to stand for preeti's mom but
she don't want to loose her now
as she loses one by one everyone . So, she takes
responsibility of preeti ' mom .*

CHAPTER EIGHT

TANYA FOUND HER LIFEMATE

Tanya is cleared about Rajkamal that he is in love . Tanya shares her Every
related things about her past relationship and about her real parents and
everything .
Rajkamal is a good guy he understands Tanya and rajkamal confessed his love
to his parents and his parents agreed . Tanya told her mom mean preeti's mom .
Tanya 's mom , why are you asking me ? You are none to me . I don't care about
you . Tanya knew well that she will react this way nothing new but preeti'd mom
had now a soft corner for Tanya as she helps a lot to both family .
Tanya 's mom replies indirectly that he is nice guy you should go for it .
Both parents were agreed Tanya and Rajkamal both had stand for each other.

They focused on there training .
Tanya has completed her training for 2 years same as rajkamal.
Both of them had engaged and back to their work . They were in same
department and had same passion . But in this field passion will be in last at first
peoples safety .
Preeti's mom accepts Tanya as her daughter and even she proud on Tanya .
She tells each every one that Tanya is her strength more than preeti was.

Tanya felt overwhelmed and went Hyderabad as District Magistrate as her duty
is on Hyderabad. Preeti's mom were also with Tanya . Tanya creates a memories
with Few unknown people and visits some places .
Tanya visits The places where Satya used to go . Rajkamal was also there with
Tanya .
Rajkamal shares her past stories with Tanya shares about
Rajkamal is Preeti 's friend . Rajkamal was felt for Preeti but preeti never loves
back to him and she had engaged and later died in a accident and all...
Tanya and Rajkamal had a same story but differentiate life and .
Tanya thinks that Satya and preeti is making them together ...

Tanya and Rajkamal gets Married together and they both had resigned the post
of Administrative officer and rajkamal became a Teacher of a school .
Tanya is also a teacher she teaches only in home . Tanya stayed for a simple and
easy lifestyle.
Tanya had twins children girl and boy , girl named as preeti and boy names as
Satya .

Quotes

*"Somewhere or sometimes They will be together again and will
creates a remarkable love story ."*

"You can connect with the author through Instagram

• @author.ashmita & @author.ashmitachakraborty

Email: chakrabortyashmita934@gmail.com "

♡
Thank you for reading this book ♡

Write yours Reviews on the stores for better work in future ♡